Make New Friends

Text and jacket art by

Rosemary Wells

Interior illustrations by

Jody Wheeler

Hyperion Books for Children

New York

LIBRARY OF CONGRESS CATALOGING-IN-PUBLICATION DATA
Wells, Rosemary.
Library of Congress Cataloging-in-Publication Data
Wells, Rosemary.
Make new friends / text and jacket art by Rosemary Wells; interior illustrations by
Jody Wheeler.—1st ed.
p.   cm. (Yoko & friends—school days)
Summary: Yoko and her classmates welcome Juanita, a new student from Texas, to
their classroom.
ISBN 0-7868-0730-X — ISBN 0-7868-1536-1 (pbk.)
[1. Friendship—Fiction. 2. Schools—Fiction. 3. Cats—Fiction. 4. Animals—
Fiction.] I. Wheeler, Jody, ill. II. Title.
PZ7.W46843 Mak 2003
[E]—dc21
2001057509

Visit www.hyperionchildrensbooks.com

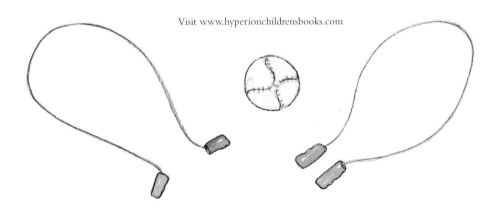

Tap, tap, tap!

"Attention, everybody!"

Mrs. Jenkins said.

Mrs. Jenkins wrote a poem

on the board.

"Can anyone read this?" she asked.

Yoko tried.

Timothy tried.

"I can read it!" said Claude.

Claude tried.

Everyone waited.

But even Claude could not

read it.

4

"I will read it out loud!"

said Mrs. Jenkins.

"Make new friends,

but keep the old.

One is silver and

the other is gold!"

"What does it mean, boys and girls?" asked Mrs. Jenkins.

"Tinfoil is silver," said Charles.

"The sunset is gold!" said Claude.

"Well," said Mrs. Jenkins,

"that's true, Charles and Claude.

Now, we have a special event today.

A new classmate has moved to
Hilltop School.

Her name is Juanita. She comes all
the way from Texas."

"Is she big or little?" asked one of
the Franks.

"Can she jump rope?" asked Charles.

"Why don't we ask her?"

said Mrs. Jenkins.

"Here she is!"

Juanita's mother brought Juanita

into Mrs. Jenkins's class.

Mrs. Jenkins played the

"Welcome" song.

Everybody sang it.

> *"Purple grow the violets!*
>
> *Green grows the grass!*
>
> *Here's a hearty welcome*
>
> *to our kindergarten class!"*

Juanita looked scared to pieces.

"Yoko, will you be the captain of
the Friend Ship, for today?"
asked Mrs. Jenkins.

"Yes," said Yoko.

Yoko took Juanita's hand

out of Juanita's mother's hand.

She sat Juanita at the

very next desk.

All morning, Juanita was too scared

to say a word.

At lunchtime, everybody sang

the "Clean Hands" song.

Juanita did not know the words.

"I will teach you," said Yoko.

By mistake the Franks sat on
Juanita's lunch.

"Don't worry," said Yoko. "I am
the captain of the Friend Ship.
That means I will take care
of you!"

Yoko stood on Mrs. Jenkins's
chair.

"Please, everybody, give something
to Juanita so that she has lunch,"
said Yoko.

Nora gave Juanita half her sandwich.

Charles gave his celery.

Grace gave Juanita her hard-boiled egg.

Fritz gave his apple.

Doris made a squeeze-cheese

tower on a plate.

And the Franks offered up their
franks and beans.

Soon Juanita had enough for four
lunches.

At playtime, Charles, Doris, and
Fritz asked Juanita if she could
jump rope double Dutch.

"I'll watch," said Juanita.

Frank asked Juanita how long

she could stand on one foot.

"*I* can do it for a long time!"

said Frank.

"Maybe I'll try it next time,"

said Juanita.

"What would *you* like to do,

Juanita?" asked Yoko.

"Just sit and watch," said Juanita.

"That's what we'll do," said Yoko.

"Because I am the captain of the

Friend Ship!"

Yoko and Juanita watched Claude

do back flips.

During snack time, Yoko taught

Juanita the words to the

"Snack Time" song.

"Too much to remember in one

day!" said Juanita.

At school-bus time, everybody
lined up for the bus.
"I have to wait for my mother,"
said Juanita. "I hope she
does not get lost!"
Juanita's voice squeaked.

"Don't cry," said Yoko. "I will wait with you, because I am the captain of the Friend Ship!"

Juanita and Yoko waited in the classroom.

"I will go and call your mother,

Yoko," said Mrs. Jenkins.

"Then she will not worry."

Yoko took out her violin.

She played "Twinkle, Twinkle,

Little Star" for Juanita, so that

Juanita would not cry.

"I wish I could do something wonderful like that," said Juanita. "Everybody in Hilltop School does something special.

Charles jumps double Dutch.

Frank stands on one foot.

"Claude can do back flips.

You play beautiful music.

But I don't do anything special,"

said Juanita.

"They must do lots of wonderful things in Texas," said Yoko.

"It's about the same in Texas," said Juanita.

"We even have the same poem about silver and gold."

"Can you read that by yourself?"

asked Yoko.

"Of course," said Juanita.

"Even Claude can't read that!"

said Yoko.

"There is nothing to it!"

said Juanita.

"My sister is the Texas spelling-bee
champion, and I know all her
words!"

"That is pretty wonderful!"

said Yoko. "See you tomorrow!"

Dear Parents,

When our children were young we lived in a small house, but we always made a space just for books. When their dad or I would read a story out loud, the TV was always off—radio and music, too—because it intruded.

Soon this peaceful half hour of every day became like a little island vacation. Our children are lifetime readers now, with an endless curiosity for the rich world waiting between the covers of good books. It cost us nothing but time well spent and a library card.

This set of easy-to-read books is about the real nitty-gritty of elementary school. There are new friends, and bullies, too. There are germs and the "Clean Hands" song, new ways of painting pictures, learning music, telling the truth, gossiping, teasing, laughing, crying, separating from Mama, scary Halloweens, and secret valentines. The stories are all drawn from the experiences my children had in school.

It's my hope that these books will transport you and your children to a setting that's familiar, yet new, a place where you can explore the exciting new world of school together.

Rosemary Wells